# Final Reckoning in Lyon

One Night of Lonely Love

Mitrajit Biswas

**Ukiyoto Publishing**

All global publishing rights are held by

**Ukiyoto Publishing**

Published in 2025

Content Copyright © Mitrajit Biswas
**ISBN 9789370090941**

All rights reserved.
No part of this publication may be reproduced, transmitted, or stored in a retrieval system, in any form by any means, electronic, mechanical, photocopying, recording or otherwise, without the prior permission of the publisher.

The moral rights of the author have been asserted.

This is a work of fiction. Names, characters, businesses, places, events, locales, and incidents are either the products of the author's imagination or used in a fictitious manner. Any resemblance to actual persons, living or dead, or actual events is purely coincidental.

This book is sold subject to the condition that it shall not by way of trade or otherwise, be lent, resold, hired out or otherwise circulated, without the publisher's prior consent, in any form of binding or cover other than that in which it is published.

www.ukiyoto.com

# Contents

| | |
|---|---:|
| The Shadows of Vieux Lyon | 1 |
| Chapter 2: Reunion of Shadows | 6 |
| Chapter 3: The Web Unravels | 12 |
| Chapter 4: Blood and Betrayal | 19 |
| Chapter 5: Siege of Bellecour | 24 |
| Chapter 6: Reckoning | 29 |
| Chapter 7: The Final Confrontation | 35 |
| Chapter 8: Aftermath and Goodbye | 40 |
| Epilogue: A New Dawn | 45 |
| *About the Author* | **49** |

# Chapter 1: The Shadows of Vieux Lyon

The cobblestone streets of Vieux Lyon lay like a mosaic of time under the soft, flickering glow of antique streetlamps. Mitrajit stepped from the taxi into a world that was both ancient and achingly alive—a city where every stone, every weathered façade, seemed to murmur secrets of a bygone era. The rhythmic clatter of his footsteps echoed against centuries-old walls as he made his way along narrow passageways that twisted like veins beneath Lyon's historic center.

In this labyrinth of history, the old-world charm of carved timber façades and ornate balconies sharply contrasted with the urgent hum of modern intelligence chatter that vibrated through his mind. Every whispered static on his earpiece, every coded message relayed through discreet channels, was a reminder that beneath the veneer of serene beauty, danger lurked in every shadow. The juxtaposition was stark: here, amid the soft luminescence of streetlamps and the faint strains of a distant accordion, the past and the present collided in an inescapable tension.

As Mitrajit navigated the labyrinthine alleys, each echo on the cobblestones stirred a cascade of memories. He recalled nights spent with Julia—those stolen moments in secret cafés tucked away from prying eyes, clandestine rendezvous in hidden alcoves behind ivy-draped walls. Laughter had mingled with whispered promises; danger and desire had interlaced in a way that made every heartbeat a defiant act of rebellion against the cold inevitability of duty. Now, each sound—the creak of an old wooden door, the distant murmur of conversation—became a bittersweet reminder of a love that once burned fiercely in the twilight of espionage.

After what seemed an eternity wandering the historical maze of Vieux Lyon, Mitrajit finally arrived at his destination—a discreet safe house nestled near the famed traboules. These secret passageways, once used by silk workers and now shrouded in modern mystery, offered refuge to those who needed to disappear from the relentless pursuit of enemies and allies alike. The safe house, an unassuming building with faded ivy clinging to its stone exterior, promised anonymity in a city where every corner was under surveillance by unseen eyes.

Inside, the atmosphere was thick with the weight of secrecy. The room was modest yet utilitarian, its walls lined with maps and tactical displays that glowed dimly in the low light. A scarred wooden table dominated the center—a silent witness to countless briefings and covert meetings. It was here that Mitrajit met Lucien, his local contact and a grizzled veteran of the DGSI. Lucien's face, creased by time and hardened by experiences, conveyed a quiet urgency as he slid a dossier across the table with a measured, almost reverent, care.

"They've planted their next move here," Lucien murmured in a gravelly voice that barely rose above a whisper. His eyes, reflecting both suspicion and determination, darted across the room as if expecting enemies to materialize from the shadows at any moment. "A cell linked to the remnants of the Khalistani network is planning a hostage crisis at the Bellecour district. And there's talk—they're working with a rogue cyber unit from Eastern Europe."

Mitrajit's hand hesitated before reaching for the dossier. As he flipped through its pages, the detailed schematics and intercepted communications unfurled like a grim tapestry—a network of clandestine plots interwoven with coded messages, financial conduits, and the dark promise of violence. Each line of data reinforced his growing certainty: nothing in Lyon was as it seemed. His instincts, honed by years of operating on the razor's edge of danger, screamed of deception and hidden threats.

But amid the cold logic of intercepted data and tactical blueprints, one name resonated with a warmth that belied the peril of the situation. Julia. Her name surfaced like an ember in the dark—a flicker of light that both comforted and tormented him. In the soft glow of the safe house, amid the rustling of papers and the low murmur of intelligence reports, his mind involuntarily wandered to memories of Julia. He remembered her gentle laughter echoing in candlelit corners of forgotten cafés, the sparkle in her eyes as they exchanged covert smiles across a crowded room, and the defiant spark of her spirit that had once made him believe in the possibility of happiness even in a life filled with danger.

The memory was not without its sting. In those recollections, every detail of her touch, every whispered secret shared in the dark, was tinged with both the sweetness of love and the bitter aftertaste of loss. Julia had been more than just a fleeting romance; she was a confidante, a partner in danger, a beacon in the darkness. And now, as her name reappeared in these clandestine briefings, it stirred a tumult of conflicting emotions—hope, regret, longing, and the unyielding resolve to do what must be done, regardless of the personal cost.

Mitrajit's jaw tightened as he resumed scanning the dossier. The schematics outlined a meticulously planned hostage crisis, pinpointing strategic locations in the Bellecour district—a place known for its bustling energy and cultural vibrancy. Yet beneath the layers of civic life lay the sinister pulse of an insurgent plan orchestrated by those who had long harbored a vendetta against the established order. The dossier described how a cell, remnants of the once-feared Khalistani network, had aligned themselves with a rogue cyber unit whose origins traced back to Eastern Europe—a partnership forged in the crucible of shared enmity and radical ambition.

Lucien's low voice broke through Mitrajit's reverie. "We're running out of time," he said. "The intel suggests that the crisis is set to unfold within the next 48 hours. Every moment we delay, the risk multiplies. I know you've seen this before, but this time it's personal."

The words struck a chord deep within Mitrajit. Personal. In his world, every mission was a matter of national security, of thwarting an enemy intent on chaos. But now, the stakes had become irreversibly entwined with the remnants of his past—Julia, the memory of their shared passion, and the uncertainty of her fate in this dangerous game. The safe house, with its stark, utilitarian decor and the ever-present hum of electronic intelligence, became a crucible where the past and the present collided.

Mitrajit rose slowly from his seat, the weight of his duty pressing upon him like a tangible force. He walked to the narrow window overlooking a courtyard where ancient stone arches cradled centuries of history.

The view was a stark reminder of the enduring spirit of Lyon—a city that had withstood wars, revolutions, and the relentless march of time. Yet beneath its picturesque facade, there lurked the specter of modern threats, a reminder that even the most beautiful places were not immune to the ravages of conflict.

In that moment of quiet reflection, the memory of Julia surged forth. He remembered a particular evening, long ago, when they had hidden in a secluded alcove behind an ivy-covered wall. The night had been filled with the soft murmur of rain against cobblestones, and the world had seemed to vanish around them. In the tender darkness, their whispered promises had filled the space between danger and desire, forging a connection that had defied both time and circumstance. Now, that connection was both his solace and his curse—a reminder of what had been lost and what might yet be reclaimed.

The dossier, now clutched in his hand, was a stark contrast to those tender memories. It was a harbinger of violence, a roadmap to chaos meticulously drawn by enemies who cared nothing for sentiment. Yet, the presence of Julia's name in the intelligence was a cruel twist of fate. It was as if destiny had conspired to remind him that the past was never truly behind him—it was an ever-present shadow, influencing every decision, every heartbeat.

Lucien's weathered face broke the silence. "We need to move, Mitrajit. The clock is ticking, and every second brings us closer to a crisis that could shatter the city." His voice carried the urgency of a man who had seen too many disasters unfold, who knew that in this world of secrets and betrayal, hesitation was tantamount to surrender.

Mitrajit nodded, his eyes hardening with resolve. "I'll coordinate with our contacts in Bellecour and mobilize our extraction teams. We cannot allow them to seize control of the situation." Yet, even as he spoke with clinical precision, a part of him longed to turn back—to retrace his steps down those hidden alleys where Julia's laughter had once filled the air, to recapture the fleeting moments of intimacy that now seemed so distant.

As he gathered his gear and prepared to leave the safe house, the dossier remained on the table, a silent testament to the storm that was coming. Its pages were filled with cold, unyielding data, yet they could not erase the warmth of a memory that continued to kindle hope in the darkest of times.

Outside, the night had deepened, and the city of Lyon pulsed with a life that was both ancient and modern a living mosaic of history and innovation, beauty and danger. Mitrajit stepped back out onto the cobblestones, the distant hum of urban life mingling with the soft strains of a violin played by a street musician in the shadows. Every step he took was a step away from the world of memories and a step into the maelstrom of a mission that would test the very limits of his resolve.

The labyrinth of Vieux Lyon was more than just a setting—it was a character, its secret corridors and hidden corners echoing with the weight of countless stories. In the quiet between heartbeats, as the city whispered its secrets to those willing to listen, Mitrajit felt the undeniable pull of fate. The memory of Julia was not merely a relic of a bygone era; it was a living ember that kindled his determination to protect what remained of a fragile, precious hope.

And so, with the dossier tucked safely under his arm and Lucien's sombre words echoing in his ears, Mitrajit disappeared into the night. The mission ahead was fraught with peril, and every shadow could harbour an enemy. Yet, he carried with him the enduring warmth of a love that had once transformed danger into passion—a love that, even amid the looming threat of chaos, promised that the light of the past could guide him through the darkness.

## Chapter 2: Reunion of Shadows

The night was deep and mysterious over Lyon as Mitrajit made his way toward a secluded courtyard off Rue Mercière. The labyrinthine passageways of this ancient quarter, lit by the warm, flickering glow of vintage streetlamps, exuded a timeless charm. Every cobblestone and weathered façade whispered echoes of history—a tapestry of bygone eras interwoven with modern secrets. The air was perfumed by the delicate scent of night-blooming jasmine, which clung to the humid darkness like an invisible veil. In this transient realm, where centuries-old architecture met the pulse of contemporary intelligence, every shadow, every whisper, carried the weight of promise and peril.

Mitrajit stepped off the taxi with measured caution, his eyes scanning the narrow alleyways. The muted sounds of distant conversations and the soft murmur of a city at rest merged with the low hum of his earpiece, through which fragments of urgent intelligence buzzed intermittently. Each intercepted message reminded him that behind the serene beauty of these ancient streets lay an undercurrent of danger—a realm where covert operations and clandestine meetings were the norm.

He moved slowly, almost reverently, along the uneven cobblestones, each step punctuated by memories that had haunted him for years. In those winding alleys, he recalled the days when laughter, danger, and passion had coexisted in fragile harmony—a time when every stolen moment in a hidden café or behind a crumbling archway had been imbued with the heady mix of love and risk. And now, that past was stirring again, like an ember reignited by a gust of wind.

At last, he arrived at a modest safe house discreetly tucked near one of the legendary traboules. The building's unassuming façade was a stark contrast to the secrets it sheltered within. Inside, dim light revealed a room lined with maps, schematics, and battered equipment—a place where time seemed to stand still, a sanctuary for those who lived in the margins of chaos. It was here that he was to await the person whose presence both comforted and tormented him.

Mitrajit found a quiet corner by a low window overlooking a shadowed courtyard. His pulse quickened with anticipation as he checked his watch. Every minute that passed deepened the mixture of hope and dread swirling in his mind. His thoughts inevitably turned to her—Julia. The mere thought of her sent a thrill through him, mingled with the bittersweet pain of memories both cherished and lost.

He recalled their clandestine meetings in hidden alcoves and secret cafés where time itself seemed to bend to their will. Their laughter, their whispered confidences in the face of danger, had forged a connection that defied the harsh realities of their world. Even now, the ghost of her presence felt palpable, as if her spirit had been waiting in the dark corners of the city for this very moment.

At exactly 11:15 PM, as if summoned by fate, a familiar silhouette emerged from the darkness. Slowly, deliberately, a figure advanced toward him. The soft rustle of fabric and the gentle sway of movement announced her arrival. As the figure drew closer, Mitrajit's breath caught in his throat. It was Julia. Her dark hair cascaded over her shoulders in loose, effortless waves, catching the ambient light and shimmering with hints of auburn. Her eyes, though guarded, held a vulnerability that spoke of untold stories and silent struggles.

"Julia," he breathed, his voice heavy with a mixture of relief, longing, and an undercurrent of sorrow. The years had etched delicate lines around her eyes—each one a testament to battles fought and survived—but they had not dimmed the quiet strength that always resided there. Yet, there was something new: a subtle radiance, a gentle softness in her expression that betrayed secret joy, and an undeniable truth that made Mitrajit's heart both swell and break simultaneously. She was pregnant.

"Mitrajit," she replied, her voice a trembling blend of warmth and apprehension. The sound of her name, spoken with such familiarity yet burdened with untold emotions, resonated deeply within him. "I never expected to see you here."

For a long moment, they simply regarded each other in the half-light of the courtyard. The air between them was thick with unspoken words and memories that had once been their refuge in a dangerous world. Then, slowly, they moved together toward a quiet corner beneath an ancient stone arch, its time-worn surface etched with the secrets of generations past. In that secluded nook, the outside world seemed to recede, leaving them suspended in a fragile moment of intimacy.

They settled into the embrace of the night. Julia's eyes glistened with unshed tears as she took a trembling breath and began to speak in a hushed, almost confessional tone. "I... I have something to tell you," she murmured, her voice barely above the rustle of the jasmine in the breeze. "I'm carrying the child of my current lover. It's a truth I have tried to keep hidden, but it's there—a reminder of a future I never anticipated."

Her words hung in the air, delicate yet heavy, like a fragile glass ornament precariously balanced on the edge of revelation. Mitrajit's heart clenched, his emotions a turbulent mix of compassion, regret, and the faint, persistent embers of a love that had once burned so brightly. The revelation was as painful as it was inevitable—a life had grown from a union that was not theirs, yet the shadows of what they had shared still loomed large.

"I tried to forget," Julia continued, her voice soft and trembling as if each word were a shard of delicate glass, "but every time danger calls, every time I hear the echo of a threat in the night, I remember how we fought side by side. I remember your unwavering courage and the way you made me believe that, even in the darkest moments, there was hope." Her eyes, reflecting both joy and sorrow, searched his face for a sign of understanding.

Mitrajit's hand trembled as it hovered near hers. For a long, agonizing moment, he could only stare into the depths of her eyes—a pool of memories where every stolen kiss, every whispered promise in the secrecy of peril, was etched into his soul. "I never stopped caring, Julia," he whispered, his voice raw with emotion. "Even if you have moved on... I can't pretend that the past doesn't bind me to you. It binds me to every moment we ever shared."

The vulnerability in his tone was palpable—a mixture of longing and the painful recognition that time had marched on, leaving both beauty and scars in its wake. Their shared history, forged in the crucible of danger and passion, now served as both a comfort and a curse. The memory of stolen kisses in rain-soaked alleys, of whispered secrets exchanged under the cover of darkness, came flooding back. It was a past that could neither be reclaimed nor entirely abandoned—a bittersweet echo that resonated with every beat of his heart.

For a long while, the world around them faded into insignificance. The gentle hum of distant traffic, the soft chirping of nocturnal creatures, and even the rustling of leaves in the cool night air all became mere background to the silent communion of two souls reunited in the midst of uncertainty. In that hushed sanctuary beneath the ancient arch, the complexities of their lives—of duty, love, and the inexorable pull of destiny—merged into one timeless moment.

"But now," she whispered, breaking the fragile silence as she pressed her hand over her rounded belly, her touch tender and filled with a quiet resolve, "my life is different. I'm tethered to a future I never imagined. Every day, I carry this new promise within me—a promise of hope and continuity that I never saw coming. And yet, when danger rises, when the world around us darkens with uncertainty, I can't help but feel drawn back to you. It's as if, no matter how far I try to move forward, the echoes of our past always find their way back into my heart."

Their eyes locked in a silent, profound acknowledgment—a moment when words were superfluous and every unspoken sentiment resonated with an intensity that belied the danger and uncertainty of their lives. In that gaze, Mitrajit saw both a future filled with uncharted possibilities and a past that he could never fully escape. The love they had once shared was not a simple memory—it was a living, breathing part of who they were, an indelible mark on their souls that defied the passage of time.

Mitrajit's thoughts swirled as he recalled the nights they had spent hidden away from the world—a world that had demanded sacrifice and secrecy. Every moment had been a battle against fate, every embrace a rebellion against the harsh realities that threatened to tear them apart.

And now, here in the quiet heart of Lyon, amidst the ancient stones and the tender scent of jasmine, those memories surged forward like a tidal wave of bittersweet recollections.

He reached out slowly, his fingertips trembling as they inched closer to hers, hesitant yet driven by an unyielding need for connection. "Julia," he murmured again, his voice laden with both yearning and resignation. "Every mission, every moment of danger we faced—it always brought me back to you. Even now, in a world that has changed so much, you remain the one constant that I cannot forget. I know you have built a new life, and I respect that. But I cannot lie to myself—I still feel what I felt then."

A tear glistened in Julia's eye as she lowered her gaze for a moment, gathering the strength to continue. "I understand, Mitrajit," she said softly, her voice quivering with both sorrow and acceptance. "I have built a future, one that I must protect for the sake of the child growing inside me. Yet, no matter how hard I try to let go of the past, there are nights like this—nights when danger whispers at the door—when I am overwhelmed by the memories of what we once were, and I find myself wishing, even if only for a fleeting moment, that things could be different."

For a long time, they sat together in the silent embrace of the ancient courtyard, the only sound the distant murmur of the city and the soft rustle of leaves in the cool night air. In that suspended moment, the painful beauty of their shared past intermingled with the uncertain promise of the future. The delicate interplay of light and shadow on their faces seemed to mirror the conflict within their hearts—a tender struggle between what was lost and what might yet be salvaged.

At last, Mitrajit spoke again, his tone resolute despite the tremor of raw emotion. "I promise you, Julia, that I will do everything in my power to protect you and the life you now carry. Even if our paths have diverged, the bond we share will always be a part of me. I will never forget the strength we found in each other in the midst of chaos, and I will carry that with me into whatever battles lie ahead."

Her hand trembled as she reached out to squeeze his, a silent gesture of both farewell and hope. "Thank you, Mitrajit," she whispered, her eyes reflecting the storm of emotions within. "In another life, perhaps our love could have found a way to flourish without the constant shadow of danger. But for now, we must accept the roles we have chosen, even if they pull us in different directions."

And so, beneath the ancient stone arch, as the night deepened and the secrets of Lyon wove around them like a delicate tapestry, Mitrajit and Julia clung to the fragile remnants of a love that had once burned brightly—a love that, despite the passage of time and the inevitability of change, would forever leave an indelible mark on their souls.

In that quiet, hallowed moment, as the past and the future converged in the soft glow of streetlamps and the tender perfume of jasmine, they found solace in the knowledge that, even if destiny forced them apart, the echoes of their shared history would forever bind them together—a bond forged in fire, shadow, and the unyielding hope that, someday, their paths might cross again.

# Chapter 3: The Web Unravels

The first blush of dawn crept over Lyon like a secret whispered in the dark, the pale light softly caressing the ornate facades of centuries-old buildings. In the early morning chill, the city exuded a quiet dignity—a living museum where every carved stone and wrought-iron balcony told tales of a bygone era. Yet beneath this veneer of beauty and history, the pulse of danger throbbed steadily, ready to disrupt the fragile calm.

Mitrajit had risen with the sun, his mind already brimming with fragments of intercepted intelligence and unsettling predictions of chaos. He made his way through narrow, dew-laden alleys toward an abandoned silk warehouse near La Croix-Rousse—a relic of Lyon's prosperous past, now repurposed as a clandestine meeting point for those who operated in the shadows. The building's crumbling brickwork and peeling paint bore silent witness to its former glory, but inside, it was transformed into a war room where the fate of many would be decided.

Inside the warehouse, dim light filtered through grimy windows, casting elongated shadows that danced on the concrete floor. Maps, blueprints, and scattered documents covered a long, scarred table at the center of the room. The air was thick with tension and the musty scent of old paper and oil, a sensory reminder of how time and history intertwined with the present. Lucien, the grizzled former DGSI operative, stood by a makeshift projector, his eyes scanning a dossier that had arrived just the previous night. His voice, low and edged with urgency, broke the silence.

"They've planted their next move right here," Lucien said, sliding a worn dossier toward Mitrajit. His calloused hand left a faint smear on the paper, a testament to years spent in covert operations. "According to these documents, the terror cell plans to seize hostages at the Grand Théâtre de Lyon during a high-profile cultural event. They intend to use the ensuing chaos to force international concessions."

Mitrajit took the dossier with deliberate care, his pulse quickening as he began to read through the meticulously detailed schematics and intercepted communications. The dossier was a labyrinth of encrypted messages, financial trails, and covert rendezvous points—a modern tapestry of terror woven with precision. One particular message, scrawled in stark red ink and barely hidden among the technical details, sent a chill down his spine:

**"When the curtain rises, the city's heartbeat will be ours."**

For a brief moment, Mitrajit's mind flashed back to previous missions—those nights of harrowing danger and calculated betrayal. The enemy's planning was as meticulous as it was merciless, combining the cold logic of cyber warfare with the raw brutality of physical infiltration. Every decision they made was laced with an intelligence that mirrored the very best of his own team's capabilities. Yet now, with the memory of Julia—her presence a bittersweet promise from a past he could neither fully embrace nor entirely forget—every new detail cut deeper, as if reminding him that the stakes were not merely geopolitical, but profoundly personal.

The warehouse fell into a focused silence as Lucien spread out a large, folded map of Bellecour on the table. With a practiced hand, he traced escape routes, entry points, and the likely positions of enemy operatives. "Our intel shows that the main operative is codenamed 'Cerberus,'" he explained in a hushed tone. "He's coordinating with a rogue cyber group based in Eastern Europe. Their plan is to merge virtual attacks with a physical takeover—locking down key systems and paralyzing the theatre when the moment is right. We have to move fast."

Mitrajit leaned over the map, his eyes narrowing as he followed Lucien's finger along the intricate network of underground tunnels and above-ground alleys that crisscrossed Bellecour. Every line and mark on the map represented a potential vulnerability or an escape route that the enemy might exploit. The gravity of the situation sank in deeper with each passing minute. He could almost feel the cold, methodical determination of Cerberus, plotting in a far-off, shadowy command center. The thought galvanized him; there was no time to waste.

## 14      Final Reckoning in Lyon

As plans were being drawn and contingencies outlined in the grim quiet of the warehouse, miles away—and in the tangled digital underbelly of Lyon—the situation was evolving on another front. Julia, whose face and gentle resilience still haunted Mitrajit's thoughts, had slipped away from their earlier secret meeting. Despite warnings from her DGSI superiors about the dangers of entanglements with former lovers, her heart refused to remain detached. Even as she navigated the maze of Lyon's cyber networks, a sense of personal duty and quiet determination propelled her forward.

In a small, cluttered office lined with humming servers and the soft glow of computer screens, Julia worked with unwavering focus. Her fingers danced over the keyboard, methodically tracing digital breadcrumbs left by the terror cell. Each keystroke was deliberate, each encrypted file she uncovered a piece of the puzzle that confirmed one grim fact: the cell was dangerously close, and time was running out. In the labyrinthine corridors of code and digital signals, she found echoes of the enemy's plan—a calculated precision that resonated with the very essence of the threat outlined in Mitrajit's dossier.

Her DGSI contact had sent her fragmented warnings, all hinting at the imminence of a coordinated attack that would exploit both cyber and physical vulnerabilities. With every decrypted message, every intercepted communication, she felt the urgency mounting. The fate of hundreds, perhaps thousands, of lives depended on the swift unraveling of this deadly web. And even as her professional mind processed the data, her heart—a secret repository of memories shared with Mitrajit—willed her to press on, driven by a sense of duty and an inescapable, lingering hope.

Back in the warehouse, as the morning wore on, the team of operatives gathered around the table with grim expressions etched on their faces. Lucien's steady, commanding voice detailed the unfolding scenario. "We must secure the perimeter around the Grand Théâtre immediately," he said, his finger still pointing at strategic choke points on the map. "If Cerberus and his team manage to execute their plan when the curtain rises, it will not only take hostages but will also cripple our ability to respond in real time. We need simultaneous teams on the ground and cyber units ready to counter any virtual sabotage."

Mitrajit absorbed every word, his mind a swirling vortex of strategic possibilities and lingering emotions. The dossier was not merely a threat; it was a gauntlet thrown at his feet—a challenge that demanded both his tactical acumen and his unyielding resolve. He recalled the coded message, its stark promise echoing in his ears: **"When the curtain rises, the city's heartbeat will be ours."** The metaphor was both elegant and chilling—a theatrical flourish for a meticulously orchestrated act of terror. It spoke of control, of commandeering not just infrastructure, but the very pulse of a city renowned for its art, culture, and resilience.

As the operatives dispersed to their respective stations, Mitrajit lingered by the map, his eyes fixed on the lines and contours that delineated Bellecour. The routes marked out for escape and infiltration were not mere tactical points; they were the battlegrounds where the coming conflict would be waged. He could almost hear the distant rumble of hostages' panicked cries, the ensuing cacophony of a city gripped by terror—a scenario he had hoped to avoid but now had to confront head-on.

The warehouse, with its cold, industrial austerity, seemed to pulse with the urgency of the unfolding operation. Lucien's seasoned voice recapitulated the plan, each word a clarion call to action. "Our window is narrow," he emphasized. "We have to neutralize the threat before the cultural event begins. Every minute we delay brings us closer to the moment when Cerberus can execute his plan. We need all available resources focused on this, and I want continuous updates from the cyber units."

Mitrajit nodded, his resolve hardening. He mentally prepared himself for the battle ahead—a confrontation that would test every fiber of his training and every remnant of his once-vibrant hope, tempered now by loss and duty. As he left the warehouse to mobilize his team, the weight of the mission pressed upon him. There was no turning back; the enemy was closing in, and every second counted.

In the quiet aftermath of the meeting, far from the tangible threat in the warehouse, Julia continued her own perilous quest. Navigating through layers of encryption and digital firewalls, she delved deeper into the intricate web spun by the terrorists. Her screen displayed a cascade of data: IP addresses, time stamps, and fragments of intercepted communications that painted a picture of a network stretching across borders and into the heart of Lyon's own digital infrastructure. Each new piece of information was a double-edged sword—a victory in the battle against terror, and a reminder of how fragile the city's heartbeat truly was.

Her heart pounded not only from the adrenaline of the chase but also from the secret hope that somewhere within these digital shadows lay a clue that would reunite her, even if only momentarily, with Mitrajit. Every encrypted file she unlocked, every trace of the rogue cyber group's signature code, affirmed one undeniable truth: the cell was near, and time was the enemy's greatest ally.

As the morning progressed, the operatives across Lyon began to converge on their designated positions. Teams were dispatched to secure key access points around the Grand Théâtre, while cyber units prepared to launch countermeasures against any attempted breaches of the city's control systems. In a temporary command center set up in a nondescript building near Bellecour, Mitrajit and his team monitored live feeds, tracking enemy movements and verifying intelligence in real time. The digital clock on the wall ticked inexorably forward, each second a reminder that the moment of reckoning was drawing ever closer.

In that charged atmosphere of calculated urgency and raw determination, Mitrajit allowed himself a fleeting moment of introspection. His mind wandered to the tender recollections of Julia—their whispered exchanges under the veil of darkness, the promise of a love that had once been his sanctuary amid the storms of duty. That bittersweet memory fueled his resolve now, transforming every strategic decision into a personal vow to protect not only the citizens of Lyon but also the fragile fragments of hope that her presence represented.

The command center buzzed with activity as technicians and field operatives communicated in rapid-fire exchanges. "All units, prepare to move on my command," Mitrajit ordered, his voice resonant and authoritative. The weight of responsibility settled on his shoulders like an armor of determination. There was no room for hesitation—not now, when the very heartbeat of the city was at risk.

Outside, as Lyon slowly awakened to an uncertain day, the intertwining threads of cyber and physical warfare were being woven into a tapestry of imminent conflict. The cultural event at the Grand Théâtre was scheduled to begin in less than three hours, a countdown that served as both a deadline and a challenge. With every update transmitted over secure channels, the picture of the enemy's plan grew clearer. Cerberus was not merely a name on a dossier; he was a ghost lurking in the digital shadows, a mastermind whose meticulous planning threatened to turn the city into a stage for terror.

The final pieces of the puzzle fell into place as Mitrajit reviewed a newly decrypted message. It was a final directive, stark and uncompromising: **"When the curtain rises, the city's heartbeat will be ours."** Those words, repeated like a dark mantra, reverberated through the command center and within Mitrajit's soul. They were both a promise and a threat—a promise of the enemy's relentless ambition and a threat that must be thwarted at all costs.

In the midst of this chaos, Julia's efforts on the cyber front yielded a breakthrough. Her screen flashed with the coordinates of a clandestine server farm tucked away in an industrial zone on the outskirts of Lyon. This facility, it appeared, was the nerve center for the rogue cyber group collaborating with Cerberus. The implications were profound: neutralizing this hub could disrupt the enemy's digital command chain, buying precious time for the ground teams.

A message pinged on her secure line—a terse, encrypted update from her DGSI liaison confirming the discovery. With a deep breath, Julia initiated a trace, following the digital breadcrumbs through layers of obfuscation and countermeasures. Each click, each command, was a battle against a clock that ticked ever faster. Yet, amidst the swirling chaos of code, her determination did not waver. The fate of Lyon— and the unspoken hope of reuniting with Mitrajit—propelled her forward.

As the day edged closer to the scheduled commencement of the cultural event, both the physical and digital fronts converged into a single, volatile nexus. Mitrajit's team was poised to intercept any move by Cerberus's operatives, and the cyber unit, under Julia's watchful eye, was ready to launch a coordinated strike against the rogue server hub. The tension in the command centre was palpable—a silent promise of action, of defiance against an enemy who sought to claim the heartbeat of a historic city.

In that crucible of modern warfare and timeless ambition, Mitrajit and his team prepared for what might be the defining battle of their careers. Every operative, every line of code, every strategic contingency was a testament to the resilience of those who dared to stand against the tide of terror. And as the clock continued its relentless march toward the fateful hour, the echoes of a long-ago love—a memory of Julia's gentle smile and unyielding spirit—remained a beacon of hope amid the encroaching darkness.

Thus, with the web of conspiracy slowly unrav5eling before them and the threat of chaos looming ever larger, Mitrajit steeled himself for the inevitable confrontation. The city of Lyon, with its ornate facades and secret undercurrents, was about to become the stage for a battle that would test every ounce of courage, ingenuity, and love left in his heart. And deep within the digital labyrinth, Julia's unwavering determination ensured that the enemy's plans would not go unchallenged—her every keystroke a silent vow to protect not only the city but also the enduring promise of their shared past.

## Chapter 4: Blood and Betrayal

Twilight had deepened into a starless night over Lyon, and the city, with its centuries-old elegance, braced for an onslaught that would shatter its serene veneer. In the heart of Bellecour, where the Grand Théâtre stood like an opulent relic from a forgotten era, vibrant lights cast shifting shadows upon its ornate entrance—a stage meticulously set for both the celebration of culture and the promise of carnage.

Without warning, the night erupted into chaos. Explosive charges, planted with sinister precision along the theatre's perimeter, detonated in a violent symphony. Shards of glass and splintered debris erupted into the cool air as terrified crowds scattered in all directions. The deafening roar of gunfire echoed through the night, a grim soundtrack to the unfolding horror. Sirens wailed in the distance as black SUVs screeched to a halt near the theatre, their engines revving as if in defiance of the imminent doom.

Mitrajit, clad in tactical gear and leading a hardened team of operatives, raced through the winding back alleys that converged on the theatre. Every sense was on high alert; his heart pounded with a mix of adrenaline and grim determination. He barked into his comms, his voice cutting through the tumult with steely authority:

"Secure the perimeter and intercept any hostiles before they breach the auditorium. I want a full sweep of every entry point now!"

The command reverberated in the tense night as his team fanned out in coordinated precision. The air was thick with shouts from soldiers and the acrid stench of burning rubber as more vehicles came to an abrupt halt. In that moment, the elegant cityscape of Lyon became a battlefield where history and modern warfare collided with unrelenting force.

Inside the grand foyer of the Théâtre, masked terrorists stormed the building with militant fervor. Their voices, hoarse and driven by radical conviction, echoed off the high, intricately adorned ceilings. The opulence of the interior—a space once designed for the celebration of art and culture—now transformed into a theater of terror. The flash of weapons, the dissonant clatter of boots on marble, and the chaotic shouts melded into a cacophony that threatened to drown out all reason.

Amid the pandemonium, Mitrajit's eyes caught a singular, chilling detail: a figure moving with deliberate grace amid the disorder—a man in a sharply tailored suit whose cold, calculating gaze swept over the scene. That figure was Cerberus, the enemy operative whose very name had become synonymous with ruthlessness. In that instant, every adrenaline-fueled memory from past missions converged into a single, brutal confrontation. Cerberus's presence was a razor-sharp reminder that the enemy was not only methodical but also imbued with a personal vendetta—a vendetta that now clashed directly with Mitrajit's own haunted past.

With no time to hesitate, Mitrajit plunged into the melee. The narrow corridors behind the stage became a claustrophobic arena for a firefight that was as sudden as it was savage. Bullets ricocheted off ancient stone and marble pillars, sending splinters of debris into the air. Mitrajit dove behind a massive marble pillar, his tactical instincts honed by years of combat. Each step forward was a battle against not only the enemy but also against the ghosts of his own history—the love he had lost, the regrets that still clawed at the edges of his resolve.

The corridors were a blur of motion: shadowy figures, the crack of gunfire, the clamor of shouts. Amid the chaos, a piercing cry cut through the clamor—a sound that resonated with both pain and determination. It was Julia. Despite the pandemonium, despite her condition and the risks inherent in her involvement, her voice came through the comms with unwavering clarity. In a tremulous yet resolute tone, she coordinated with the local French operatives, ensuring that every critical point of the operation was covered.

"Hold your position, Julia," Mitrajit's commlink crackled with urgency as he fought his way through a corridor riddled with debris. "We're almost at the control room. I need you to keep the enemy from overrunning our lines."

Her response was immediate, laced with the familiar blend of caution and fierce resolve that he had once known so well: "I'm on my way—don't do anything reckless." The exchange, brief as it was, carried an emotional weight that belied the danger of the moment. In that fleeting communication, the distance between them shrank to nothing more than shared memories and unspoken promises.

Every footfall, every breath, became a testament to the high stakes of the night. Mitrajit moved through the corridors like a shadow, his mind a kaleidoscope of past battles and the present peril. He remembered the nights when Julia's laughter had punctuated the darkness, a sound so pure that it made him believe even in the face of impossible odds. Now, each step forward was driven by that same hope—a hope that he might yet protect what remained of a love that had once set his heart ablaze.

As the firefight intensified, the corridors of the ancient theatre became a battleground for not only life and death but for redemption. Mitrajit's team exchanged rapid-fire commands as they cleared room after room. Explosive charges rattled the structure, sending plumes of dust and sparks cascading along the stone walls. Amid the chaos, the tailored figure of Cerberus emerged from the haze, engaging in a deadly dance with Mitrajit. The clash of their wills was swift and brutal; each move was calculated, every parry a silent testament to the years of training that had led them to this moment. Cerberus's eyes, as cold as the winter's bite, reflected a single-minded focus on domination, while Mitrajit's, fueled by a haunted determination, burned with the desire to right the wrongs of his past.

Time seemed to slow in the narrow back corridors, every second laden with the potential for life-altering consequences. Bullets whizzed past, barely missing their mark as Mitrajit darted from cover to cover. The acrid smell of gunpowder mingled with the ancient musk of the theatre's old stones. In that confined space, every heartbeat reverberated like a drum of war, echoing with memories of battles fought and promises unfulfilled.

Then, amidst the relentless barrage of gunfire, another sound emerged—a desperate, piercing cry that cut through the din of combat. It was unmistakably Julia, her voice quivering with a blend of fear and steely determination. For a heartbeat, the chaos paused as her voice reached him over the commlink, the sound a lifeline in a sea of violence.

"Keep your focus, Mitrajit," she urged, her tone both tender and commanding. "I'm coordinating with the French operatives. I won't let them break through. Just... hold on a little longer."

Her words, carried over the static-filled channel, imbued him with renewed strength. Every shouted command, every carefully executed maneuver was underscored by the knowledge that she was out there, fighting as fiercely as he was—her presence a bittersweet reminder of a shared past that had shaped both their lives. In that moment, the battlefield transformed into something more than a simple clash of forces; it became a crucible where old wounds and new alliances converged.

Mitrajit's gaze swept across the corridor as he advanced toward the control room—a mission-critical objective that could turn the tide of the night. Behind him, the relentless firefight continued, punctuated by explosions that sent tremors through the ancient walls. The intensity of the battle was matched only by the intensity of his own emotions. Every moment in that confined space was a battle not just against the enemy, but against the pull of memories that threatened to unbalance him—memories of a love lost, of whispered promises in the dark, and of the inescapable connection he still felt for Julia.

As he neared the control room, Mitrajit's commlink crackled again with Julia's voice—a brief, urgent message that made his heart race even faster. "Mitrajit, I'm closing in. I've secured the southern corridor. Just a little further, and we'll have the system under control. Don't let your guard down." Her words were a mixture of reassurance and a stark reminder of the risks that lay ahead.

In the flickering half-light of the theatre's back corridors, amid the echoing blasts and the chaos of combat, every whispered command, every exchanged glance, carried an emotional weight that transcended the mere tactical significance of the mission. It was a moment where duty and personal history collided—a moment where every bullet fired, every step taken, was infused with the memory of what they had once shared, and the promise of what they could still fight for.

Mitrajit, driven by the unyielding need to protect both the hostages and the flickering vestiges of his own past, pressed forward with a determination that bordered on the heroic. Each maneuver was calculated, each decision made in the crucible of combat that fused the past with the present. As he reached the threshold of the control room, the cacophony of the firefight crescendoed, the air heavy with the acrid tang of smoke and the metallic scent of spilled blood.

In that climactic moment, as the echoes of gunfire and the shouts of combatants receded into a tense silence, Mitrajit steeled himself for what lay ahead. The battle was far from over, and the specter of Cerberus still loomed large in the chaotic darkness. But with Julia's voice guiding him through the storm—a beacon of hope amidst the relentless tide of blood and betrayal—he knew that every sacrifice, every risk, was a step toward reclaiming not just the city's heartbeat, but a fragment of the love he had once lost.

The night was alive with the struggle of heroes and villains, of duty and desire, of memories that refused to fade even in the face of relentless violence. And as Mitrajit continued his desperate march toward the control room, every beat of his heart echoed with the promise that, no matter the cost, he would protect the fragile spark of hope that Julia represented—until the very end.

# Chapter 5: Siege of Bellecour

Inside the oppressive darkness of the Grand Théâtre's auditorium, terror had taken hold. Dozens of hostages were herded like cattle into a confined space where hope was rapidly diminishing. The once-illuminated stage—designed to showcase the brilliance of human artistry—now lay shrouded in a dim, eerie light. That pallid glow was intermittently shattered by the harsh glare of flashlights, wielded by enemy operatives whose cold eyes were fixed on their next move. Overhead, the omnipresent hum of remote-controlled devices—sophisticated, rigged to detonate at a moment's notice—served as a menacing reminder that time was slipping away.

Mitrajit's team had already spread out in tight formation along the corridors that snaked around the auditorium. Every step they took was measured with the weight of impending doom—a desperate gamble between life and death. In the silence punctuated by hurried footsteps and whispered orders, the ticking of a clock reverberated in every operative's mind, reminding them that the terrorists' plan was about to reach its deadly crescendo.

## The Methodical Advance

With a grim determination etched on his face, Mitrajit led his team forward. They advanced methodically, clearing one corridor after another. Each room they entered was a potential minefield—a place where enemy operatives lurked in the shadows, waiting to spring their trap. As they pushed through the chaos, shattered glass and scattered fragments of hastily scribbled plans littered the floor. Every broken shard was a silent witness to the violence that had already erupted and the carnage that might yet come.

"Clear left! Clear right!" Mitrajit barked into his comms, his voice a razor of command amidst the cacophony of explosions and panicked shouts. His team, seasoned in the art of covert combat, moved with swift precision. One by one, enemy operatives fell—neutralized in a dance of bullets and close-quarters combat. The corridor became a blur of desperate struggles, where every encounter was a test of grit and skill.

As the team pressed forward, Mitrajit focus narrowed on a trail that led to the backstage control room. It was there that the enemy's nerve centre was rumoured to be hidden—a place from which the terrorists orchestrated the siege on Bellecour. The passage was lined with debris: glass that glinted in the sparse light, torn sheets of paper bearing fragments of maps and orders, and the remnants of hastily abandoned equipment. Every piece of evidence testified to a struggle that had been fought and planned with ruthless precision.

## The Confrontation with Cerberus

At last, Mitrajit reached the threshold of the control room. The heavy door, scarred with bullet holes and splintered wood, creaked open under his firm push. Beyond lay a small chamber, dimly lit by the flickering light of malfunctioning monitors and the cold glare of emergency lamps. And there, standing amid the chaos, was the man he had been dreading to face.

Cerberus. His very presence was as chilling as the name suggested—a man whose icy veneer of composure barely masked the fury of a mastermind. Dressed in a perfectly tailored suit that contrasted sharply with the disorder around him, Cerberus exuded an air of calculated menace. His eyes, cold and unyielding, scanned the room as though he were both judge and executioner.

Mitrajit's pulse surged as he stepped forward, every muscle tensed for the impending clash. "You think you can dictate the fate of an entire city?" he hissed, his voice low, dangerous, and thick with the accumulated weight of past betrayals and lost promises.

Cerberus allowed a self-assured smirk to cross his features as he casually reloaded his pistol, each click echoing like a death knell. "Fate is a construct, Mr. Mitrajit. Tonight, we rewrite the rules," he replied, his tone mocking and icy. In that charged moment, the control room became the stage for a brutal confrontation—a collision of wills that had been building for years.

Without a moment's hesitation, the ensuing duel erupted into a maelstrom of violence. Fists flew and bodies twisted in a deadly ballet as Mitrajit and Cerberus engaged in a fierce hand-to-hand combat. The clash was swift and brutal—a blend of explosive manoeuvres and desperate gunfire. Every lunge, every parry was laden with the weight of personal history: the ghosts of battles past, the echo of promises once made, and the bitter taste of fractured loyalties. Cerberus lunged repeatedly, his movements a blend of precision and fury, while Mitrajit countered with the raw determination of a man fighting for more than just survival.

Time itself seemed to slow as their struggle reached its apex. Amid the fury of clenched fists and the crack of splintering bones, the control room became an arena where every clash resonated with the intensity of a personal vendetta. Then, as Cerberus staggered backward from a particularly punishing blow, Mitrajit seized a fallen submachine gun from the ground. With a forceful thrust, he pinned Cerberus against the cold, scarred wall, his grip unyielding.

"It's over," Mitrajit growled, his voice merging with the distant wail of approaching sirens—a sound that heralded the end of chaos and the hope of order. The subdued form of Cerberus slumped against the wall, his defiant eyes dimming as the battle within him ceased. With the enemy operative now in his control, Mitrajit immediately transmitted a secure message to command: all remaining terrorists were to be contained, and no further hostages would be allowed to suffer.

## Aftermath of the Battle

Outside the control room, the firefight continued to rage—a desperate struggle for survival that had engulfed the theatre. The deafening noise of sporadic gunfire and the relentless clamor of shouts filled the vast corridors. Yet even as the tide of battle began to turn, the night was far from over. Every second was a reminder that the enemy's tactics were as unpredictable as they were ruthless.

Over the comms, Mitrajit thoughts were suddenly interrupted by a softer, yet no less urgent, voice. It was Julia. Her voice, transmitted through the static, was softer now—a gentle counterpoint to the explosive violence that surrounded them. "Mitrajit, I'm almost through. The hostages are safe," she reported, her tone steady despite the turmoil. "But there's one more explosive rigged to the main chandelier. I need you to—"

Before her warning could be completed, a secondary explosion tore through the auditorium. The shockwave rippled through the building, sending a rain of dust and debris cascading from above. In the chaotic aftermath, the once-grand auditorium was plunged into disarray—a swirling maelstrom of smoke, sparks, and anguished cries.

In an instant of razor-sharp instinct, Mitrajit sprang into action. Amid the swirling chaos, he shielded a group of trembling hostages, ushering them toward the relative safety of a side exit. Every heartbeat hammered in his ears, every breath a mixture of adrenaline and dread. His mind raced with the knowledge that this was not the end of the terror that had been unleashed—it was merely the prelude to a final reckoning.

Outside, the echoes of the secondary explosion mingled with the distant rumble of emergency services converging on the scene. The theatre, now a maelstrom of violence and ruin, bore the scars of a calculated onslaught. Yet even amid the devastation, Mitrajit resolve burned brighter than ever. He knew that every moment of delay, every hesitation, could cost more lives. As he continued to coordinate the rescue, his thoughts were haunted by the silent promise he had made to protect those who could not protect themselves.

Every command he issued was a lifeline—a desperate plea for order in the chaos. "Secure that corridor!" he roared into the comms, his voice steady despite the whirlwind of destruction. "Get the hostages out! We need to hold this position until the bomb squad arrives!" His words were met with the rapid responses of his team—a symphony of disciplined, courageous replies that cut through the dissonance of terror.

As the dust began to settle, Mitrajit paused for a fleeting moment, his eyes scanning the devastation that lay before him. The grandeur of the Grand Théâtre had been transformed into a battleground—a tragic collision of art, culture, and violence. Amid the shattered remnants of elegance, the fight for survival continued with unrelenting urgency.

In that moment, his mind flashed to the voices of the hostages, the frantic commands of his team, and, most piercingly, the echo of Julia's words over the comms. Her voice was a beacon in the darkness—a reminder that even during overwhelming carnage, there existed a thread of hope that could not be severed.

Mitrajit gripped the submachine gun tighter as he surveyed the scene. Though Cerberus lay defeated at his feet, the battle for Bellecour was far from over. The terrorists had not been eradicated; they were regrouping, preparing for the next act of their deadly plan. With grim determination, he transmitted one final, resolute message to command: "Contain all hostiles. No further casualties. We hold Bellecour at all costs."

In the quiet lull that followed the chaos of the secondary explosion, every operative in the theatre understood that the night's horrors were only a precursor to the final reckoning that lay ahead. For Mitrajit, every echo of gunfire, every shattered remnant of the chandelier, was a reminder of the price of betrayal—a price measured not just in blood and shattered dreams, but in the relentless fight for a future free from terror.

As he moved back into the heart of the ruined auditorium to secure the last remaining hostages, his thoughts lingered on the gravity of the night's events. The Grand Théâtre, once a symbol of artistic grandeur, had become a crucible where loyalty, courage, and love were tested in the most brutal of ways. And during that crucible, Mitrajit found his own resolve hardening like tempered steel—each step forward a defiant promise to those who had suffered, and a silent vow to never let the darkness claim victory.

With the hostages safely evacuated and his team consolidating their positions, the echoes of the night's violence gradually began to fade. Yet, the memory of every bullet fired, every desperate plea, and every shattered fragment of hope would linger long after the last siren had faded into the distance. For in the ruins of Bellecour, amid the blood and betrayal, Mitrajit knew that the final reckoning was not merely an end, but the beginning of a long and arduous journey toward redemption—and perhaps, in the silent spaces between heartbeats, toward the possibility of reclaiming a lost love.

# Chapter 6: Reckoning

Outside the ravaged theatre, the night had finally surrendered to an inky early dawn. The chaos of the previous hours had ebbed away into a heavy, solemn stillness. Emergency services—ambulances, fire trucks, and police vehicles—converged on the scene with wailing sirens that mingled with the distant echo of collapsing structures. Makeshift triage centers had been hastily erected in nearby courtyards and parking lots, their white tarps fluttering against a backdrop of destruction. Amid the ruin, the Grand Théâtre stood as a shattered monument to a once-glorious past, its ornate features marred by explosions and bullet holes.

Mitrajit stood at the periphery of the scene, leaning against a cold concrete wall. His eyes, still alert and calculating, were fixed on the broken remnants of a once vibrant cultural landmark. Yet in his mind, a separate battle raged—a tumult of conflicting emotions that rendered his recent victory against Cerberus hollow and bittersweet. Though he had subdued the enemy mastermind, the cost of that victory was etched into every scar on his soul.

He thought back to the relentless firefight, the savage melee that had forced him to confront not only his enemy but also the ghosts of his past. Now, the silence of dawn brought with it the stark realization of what had been lost and what might yet be reclaimed. As wounded civilians were carried away and paramedics worked with urgent efficiency, his thoughts turned to Julia—the woman whose face, illuminated by the glow of a solitary streetlamp, had haunted his dreams and driven his every action.

Some time later, in a quiet courtyard tucked behind the battered façade of the theatre, Mitrajit finally found her. The space was small and secluded, its ancient stone walls softened by the gentle light of a lone streetlamp that cast long, trembling shadows on the worn cobblestones. Here, away from the clamorous urgency of the emergency response, time seemed to slow, offering a brief respite from the relentless barrage of violence and duty.

Julia emerged from the darkness as if conjured by his longing. Her features, though etched by fatigue and sorrow, retained an ethereal beauty. The soft glow of the lamp traced delicate lines on her face, highlighting the determination in her tired eyes. Her presence exuded both vulnerability and resolve. Slowly, she stepped forward, her voice barely above a whisper, laden with remorse.

"I'm sorry," she said, her tone trembling with a mixture of sorrow and regret. "I'm so sorry for the pain I've caused, for the confusion of our hearts. I never meant to put you in harm's way."

Mitrajit's gaze remained steady, though his heart ached with unspoken words. The quiet intensity of the moment carried the weight of shared history—the laughter, the promises made in secret, the nights spent side by side, facing danger head-on. "I know," he replied softly, his voice catching with the unsaid. "Every mission, every battle—it always seems to lead back to you, Julia. I thought that time might heal the wounds, but the truth is, I've never stopped."

Her hand, delicate yet resolute, came to rest over her rounded belly. It trembled slightly, betraying the gravity of her new reality. "I'm carrying another man's child now," she confessed, her voice heavy with resignation. "I have a life and a future I must protect… yet, in the quiet moments when the world falls silent, my heart still clings to what we had."

For a heartbeat, the world around them fell into a deep, suspended silence. The distant wail of sirens, the soft murmur of emergency workers, even the rustling of leaves in the early morning breeze—all seemed to vanish, leaving only the fragile connection between them. In that quiet, private space, the shared pain of past betrayal and the lingering warmth of old love intermingled in an almost tangible embrace.

But as the silence deepened, a new sound cut through the calm—a sharp, insistent beeping over Mitrajit's commlink. His eyes narrowed as he read the incoming intelligence update. The message was brief but alarming: a hidden faction within the terror network had reactivated an encrypted signal—one that could trigger a citywide cyber assault remotely. The mastermind behind this final gambit was still at large, concealed within the labyrinthine depths of Lyon's underworld.

The weight of the new threat pressed down on him instantly, and his eyes met Julia's with a mixture of urgency and reluctant resolve. "We have to move," Mitrajjit said, his tone carrying the gravity of a man torn between duty and the fragile remnants of personal desire. "This isn't just about us anymore—it's about saving countless lives."

Julia hesitated for a long moment, her eyes reflecting a turmoil that mirrored his own. Torn between the duty imposed on her by DGSI and the powerful pull of emotions that still bound her to him, she finally nodded slowly. "I'll help," she said, her voice low yet resolute. "I have contacts here at DGSI who can assist us. But promise me one thing, Mitrajit—you have to come back to me. Promise me you'll let go of the past just enough to build a future."

Her plea was raw and vulnerable, carrying the unspoken hope of what might have been if fate were kinder. In that delicate exchange, the unspoken promises of a shared past and the uncertain hope of a future intermingled in the dim light of dawn.

Without a moment's hesitation, they moved together from the safety of the courtyard. The city was stirring with the promise of a new day, yet every narrow street and shadowed alleyway of Lyon now bore the imprint of impending confrontation. Side by side, they raced through the winding passages, their footsteps echoing against ancient stone as they navigated the labyrinthine network of Lyon's streets.

Mitrajit's mind raced as fast as his feet. Each step was laden with the memory of past battles and the bitter taste of unresolved regrets. The city, normally a mosaic of beauty and history, had transformed overnight into a chessboard of danger and desperation. Every hidden corner might conceal enemy operatives, every darkened alley might hide a trap. And yet, amidst the chaos and uncertainty, his resolve remained unshaken. The reactivation of the encrypted signal was not merely an operational setback—it was a clarion call, a final challenge from an enemy whose cunning and cruelty seemed to know no bounds.

As they sprinted along a narrow lane, the first light of dawn casting an eerie glow on the dew-covered pavement, Mitrajit's thoughts turned to the future. He could not ignore the magnitude of the threat that lay ahead. The possibility of a citywide cyber assault was a dire one—one that could cripple not only Lyon but potentially spread chaos far beyond its borders. His mind, ever the battlefield for conflicting loyalties, acknowledged that the path forward would demand sacrifice and unfaltering commitment to duty. Yet, the thought of Julia—of her smile, her courage, the love they had once shared—lent him strength and hope in equal measure.

In a brief moment of respite along a deserted boulevard, they halted to catch their breath. The world around them was slowly awakening; the first rays of sun illuminated the ornate facades of historic buildings, while the remnants of violence from the night before lay scattered like shattered dreams. In that quiet interlude, the tension between duty and desire hung palpably in the air.

"Mitrajit," Julia said softly, her eyes searching his with a mix of longing and determination. "We stand at a crossroads. We must stop this new threat, no matter the cost. But I need you to know—every battle we fight, every sacrifice we make, is a step towards healing. I want to believe that one day, after all the chaos has subsided, we might find a way back to each other."

Her words resonated deeply within him, stirring memories of long-forgotten promises and tender moments shared in the heat of danger. "I promise," he replied, his voice steady despite the whirlwind of emotions surging within him. "I will see this through. I'll stop this threat—and then, if fate allows, I'll come back to you. We will rebuild something new from the ashes of what we once had."

Their hands clasped tightly as they resumed their race through the labyrinth of Lyon's streets. Every corner they turned, every dark passage they traversed, was fraught with peril. The city itself seemed to pulse with an undercurrent of menace—a silent witness to the unfolding drama of duty, love, and betrayal. As they reached a rendezvous point near an old metro station, Mitrajit's commlink buzzed again with urgent updates from his command center. The reactivated encrypted signal had been traced to a nondescript building in a forgotten industrial quarter—a hidden nerve center for the terror network's cyber operations.

"We have confirmation," Mitrajjit said into the commlink, his voice a mix of resolve and fatigue. "The enemy's command center is located at the old textile mill on the outskirts. We need to secure that facility before the cyber assault is launched. Time is running out."

Julia's eyes flashed with determination as she absorbed the gravity of the situation. "I'll coordinate with my DGSI contacts and get a team in position. We can disrupt their network from within. Just—promise me, Mitrajit, that you'll come back to me once this is over."

Her plea, though laden with duty, carried a heartfelt vulnerability that made his chest tighten with both love and sorrow. "I promise," he whispered, his tone imbued with a sincerity that left no room for doubt. "We'll stop this, Julia. And when the city is safe, I'll find my way back to you—no matter what it takes."

Together, they plunged into the unfolding crisis, their figures merging with the growing bustle of Lyon as emergency lights, military vehicles, and covert operatives converged on the enemy's last stronghold. The dawn had fully broken now, casting a cold, unforgiving light on a city still reeling from the scars of violence. Amid the organized chaos, Mitrajit led his team toward the industrial quarter, every step measured, every moment crucial.

In the midst of their hurried advance, Mitrajit's inner battle raged on. He recalled every memory of Julia—their clandestine meetings, the laughter shared in secret corners of the world, and the pain of their parting. That love, though marred by betrayal and sacrifice, was a beacon that now guided him through the darkest hours. It reminded him that even in the shadow of overwhelming duty, there remained something profoundly human worth fighting for.

As they neared the derelict textile mill, the building loomed like a specter from a forgotten era, its once-proud architecture now a crumbling relic beset by decay and neglect. Yet within its walls, the enemy had built a hub of digital warfare—a place where chaos was not just planned, but meticulously orchestrated. Mitrajit's team quickly surrounded the perimeter, their movements synchronized like a well-rehearsed dance. Every operative knew the stakes: if this facility fell, the terror network's final gambit would plunge the entire city into darkness.

The tension was palpable as they prepared to breach the building. In those final moments before action, Mitrajit's thoughts returned once more to Julia—the promise in her eyes, the hope in her voice. With every beat of his heart, he vowed silently that no matter what the coming battle demanded, he would protect not only the city but also the fragile spark of love that had ignited a fire within him so long ago.

"Team, move in!" Mitrajjit commanded, his voice resolute and unwavering. The operatives surged forward, disappearing into the yawning entrance of the old mill. The sound of footsteps, whispered orders, and the rustle of tactical gear filled the air as they closed in on the enemy's lair.

Outside, amidst the tumult of the unfolding assault, Julia's voice came through once more over the commlink—a final reminder of the bond that had brought them together and would, she hoped, eventually pull them apart from the precipice of despair. "Keep your focus, Mitrajit," she urged softly. "I'm with you, even if we're apart. Just remember our promise."

Her words, carried on the crisp morning air, fortified his resolve. As the team penetrated deeper into the mill, the final confrontation with the enemy's cyber operatives loomed large—a reckoning that would determine not only the fate of Lyon but also the future of the fragile, wounded hope that had brought him to this moment.

With the new threat still pulsing like a dark heartbeat beneath the city, Mitrajit led his team into the heart of the industrial complex, prepared to do whatever it took to end the terror network's reign. Every moment was a reminder of the sacrifices made and the love that lingered despite the cost. And as the battle for the city's soul reached its climax, he clung to the promise that, when the dust finally settled, he would return to Julia—a promise forged in the crucible of chaos, tempered by duty, and sustained by an undying love.

# Chapter 7: The Final Confrontation

Under the cold light of a pre-dawn sky, Lyon's underbelly revealed itself in a way few ever witnessed. Deep beneath the forgotten remnants of an abandoned silk mill—its once-proud walls now succumbing to time and neglect—an underground data center pulsed with an eerie, almost otherworldly glow. The facility, hidden in plain sight beneath crumbling brick and rusted iron, had been transformed into a nerve center of terror. Here, the final enemy waited: a room lined with monitors and blinking lights that cast long, wavering shadows across concrete floors stained with memories of past battles.

Mitrajit moved silently along the narrow corridors of the data center, his elite team flanking him in tight formation. Every step was measured; every breath was held as though the very air were laden with danger. The monitors around him displayed streams of encrypted code, scrolling inexorably toward a deadline. If activated, the code would launch a cyber assault so devastating that it would cripple Lyon's infrastructure—and the shockwaves would reverberate far beyond the borders of France.

Accompanying him was Julia, now temporarily assigned to DGSI's rapid response unit. The intensity of her presence cut through the oppressive tension like a beacon of both hope and heartache. Her eyes, focused and unwavering, betrayed the personal cost of the mission—a cost that weighed heavily on both her and Mitrajit. Though they had worked together before, the unspoken history between them now mingled with the urgency of the present, their professional purpose tempered by the raw emotions that had never fully faded.

They pressed deeper into the labyrinth of the data center. The corridor walls, lined with pipes and exposed wiring, hummed with the low drone of machinery that never truly slept. Every flicker of a monitor and every beeping alert heightened the palpable sense of doom. It was as though the facility itself was alive—a malevolent presence waiting to unleash chaos.

At the heart of this underground lair, Mitrajjit and his team reached the control room. Here, a bank of monitors glowed with the unmistakable pulse of encrypted lines of code. Before them, a flickering screen sprang to life, revealing a ghostly figure whose visage was masked by shadow and static. The figure, known only as "Le Fantôme," spoke in a modulated, cold tone that resonated through the quiet tension of the room.

"You're too late, Agent Mitrajjit," Le Fantôme intoned, his voice detached and unnervingly calm. "The city will fall into darkness, and with it, the hope of your lost love." The threat was delivered with clinical precision—a declaration that held no room for error, no space for mercy.

For a heartbeat, time seemed to suspend as the weight of those words bore down on Mitrajjit. But there was no time for despair. Almost immediately, the silence shattered with the roar of gunfire and the cacophony of shouts. The operatives stationed around the control room sprang into action as a fierce firefight erupted. Metal clashed with metal, and bullets ricocheted off reinforced surfaces in a deadly symphony of chaos.

Mitrajit's focus narrowed as he led his team through the ensuing melee. In the chaos, he could barely register the relentless barrage of enemy fire, the echoing blasts, and the shattering of glass. Instead, every sense was fixated on the mission: to prevent the enemy from activating the terminal that controlled the impending cyber assault. The fate of Lyon depended on it.

Amid the swirl of combat, Mitrajit caught sight of Julia, who was coordinating with local French operatives via her commlink. Even as enemy operatives advanced, her voice emerged—calm yet resolute—cutting through the din of destruction. "Mitrajit, I'm almost through. The hostages are safe," she reported, her tone steady despite the ferocity of the battle around her. "But there's one more explosive rigged to the main chandelier. I need you to—" Before she could finish, a secondary explosion ripped through the control room, sending a shockwave that sent debris and sparks flying in every direction.

In that heart-stopping moment, as dust and chaos enveloped him, Mitrajjit acted purely on instinct. He lunged forward, shielding a group of hostages with his body and dragging them to safety behind a collapsed support beam. His heart pounded not just with the adrenaline of combat, but with the personal terror of nearly losing Julia again.

"Julia!" he bellowed into the commlink, the desperation in his voice slicing through the static. There was a brief pause—a second that stretched into an eternity—before her voice responded, laced with both pain and determination. In that moment, amid the swirling darkness and chaos, Mitrajjit glimpsed the fierce resolve in her eyes. Even as she risked everything to shield him from a collapsing beam—a sacrifice that nearly cost her life—she remained the embodiment of strength he had long admired.

The firefight raged on in the corridors of the data center. Amid the chaos, Mitrajjit and his team fought with a mixture of acrobatic finesse and raw, brutal efficiency. Every movement was a calculated step toward dismantling the enemy's network. As he advanced toward the terminal controlling the cyber assault, sparks flew from malfunctioning wires and shattered screens, casting eerie, dancing lights upon his determined face.

Reaching the terminal, Mitrajjit's fingers flew over the keys with a speed that belied the tension in his veins. It was as if each keystroke were a solemn vow—a promise not only to protect the city from impending doom but also to preserve the memory of all they had once shared. The code before him was a labyrinth of encryption and potential destruction; one misstep could spell catastrophe. But with every line of code he disabled, every countermeasure he overrode, he could almost feel the weight of the enemy's ambitions fading.

Outside the control room, the battle continued to surge. Reinforcements were pouring in, and the sound of distant sirens melded with the relentless clatter of combat. Yet within the confines of that critical space, every moment was a struggle against time—a race to prevent the trigger of a digital apocalypse. The terminal's screen, once a glowing beacon of lethal potential, began to dim as Mitrajjit entered the final line of code. With a final, decisive keystroke, the monitors went dark, signaling that the cyber assault had been neutralized.

For a long, suspended moment, the silence in the control room was overwhelming—a heavy, breathless pause in the midst of chaos. The threat had been contained, but the cost was etched in every drop of sweat, every tear shed by the brave souls who had fought alongside him.

Slowly, as reinforcements secured the data center and enemy operatives were rounded up, Mitrajjit turned toward the figure that had been at the center of his heartache and hope—Julia. In the flickering, uncertain light of emergency lamps, her face was etched with exhaustion, sorrow, and a fierce determination that shone despite the scars of the battle. Her eyes, rimmed with dirt and tears, met his with an intensity that communicated all the unspoken words between them.

"I did it," she whispered, her voice trembling with both relief and the lingering echoes of the confrontation. "I helped save Lyon."

The words, simple and profound, hung in the charged air. Mitrajjit's heart swelled with a torrent of emotion. Gently, as if afraid to shatter the delicate hope that still lingered between them, he reached out and brushed a stray tear from her cheek. "You saved so much more than a city tonight," he murmured, his voice thick with emotion and the weight of years of longing.

For a heartbeat, the battlefield—filled with the din of receding chaos, the echo of distant sirens, and the soft hum of subdued equipment—seemed to vanish. In that intimate, fragile moment, the only reality was the raw, unspoken truth that bound them: a love forever transformed by duty and sacrifice, one that had been tempered by the fires of battle and the bitter taste of loss.

Yet, even as the final vestiges of the threat were being contained and the enemy's plans were unraveled line by line, Mitrajjit knew that the scars of this night would run deep. The data center, the abandoned silk mill, and the ruined corridors would forever bear witness to a confrontation where the fate of a city—and the remnants of a love once thought lost—hung in the balance.

As the first light of dawn began to break through the grimy windows, illuminating the ruin and chaos with a pale, unforgiving glow, Mitrajjit and Julia stood together in the aftermath. Around them, the shattered remnants of the digital war receded into silence, but in their eyes burned the knowledge that the fight for their future was only just beginning.

With the threat neutralized and the monitors dark, Mitrajjit exhaled a ragged breath—a sound that mingled relief with the heavy sorrow of sacrifice. He knew that no victory could erase the cost of what had been lost, nor could it mend the wounds of a past that would forever linger in the quiet spaces between heartbeats.

Yet, in that moment of tentative calm, as Julia's trembling hand found his and their eyes locked in a silent promise of what might be, there was a spark—a fragile, glimmering hope that even in the darkness, love could still find a way to survive.

The final confrontation was over, but its echoes would reverberate through the corridors of their souls for years to come. Amid the ruin of the data center, as the morning light bathed the once-forgotten underground facility in a somber glow, Mitrajjit vowed that no matter what new challenges lay ahead, he would protect not only the city of Lyon but also the tender hope that had once bound him to Julia—a hope forged in the crucible of sacrifice, duty, and a love that would endure beyond the battlefield.

And so, as reinforcements secured the area and the remnants of the enemy were rounded up, Mitrajjit and Julia stood side by side in the fading light of the emergency lamps, their hearts beating in unison—a final, silent reckoning with fate, and a promise that even the deepest scars could someday give way to healing.

# Chapter 8: Aftermath and Goodbye

The days that followed the chaos were filled with a quiet, tentative rebuilding. As Lyon slowly stitched together the wounds of that harrowing night, a fragile peace began to settle over the city. The terror network, once a looming specter over Bellecour, had been decimated; its final whispers had been silenced by the courage of those who refused to yield. Yet for Mitrajjit, the victory bore a heavy, personal cost that no celebration could ever truly erase.

*Morning in the City of Resilience*

In the early light of a crisp morning, the streets of Lyon exuded an air of subdued optimism. The ancient facades, once scarred by explosions and the bitter tang of gunfire, now wore a tentative look of renewal. Café tables spilled onto sidewalks along the banks of the Rhône, and the gentle murmur of conversations blended with the soft clink of porcelain. Amidst this normalcy, the remnants of last night's violence still lingered in the memories of those who had survived.

At a quiet café along the river, Mitrajjit sat alone at a small, weathered table. The cup of coffee before him had long since grown cold—a silent testament to the hours lost in reflection. He stared out across the water, watching as the city bustled with the indifferent rhythms of daily life, oblivious to the secrets of its dark past. Every ripple in the Rhône, every glimmer of sunlight on the water, recalled fragments of the night's terror—and the faces of those he had fought so hard to save.

Mitrajjit's mind drifted to Julia. In those quiet moments, her laughter, her defiant spirit, and the bittersweet promise of a future that could never truly be theirs swirled in his thoughts. He remembered the final embrace in the underground data center, the silent exchange of tears, and the tender words that had passed between them in the midst of chaos. Each memory was both a comfort and a wound—a reminder of love lost amid the relentless demands of duty.

*Reflections in Solitude*

As he sat in solitude, Mitrajjit's heart felt heavy with the burden of every mission, every sacrifice. He recalled how the final confrontation had ended in the cold, harsh light of dawn: the enemy vanquished, the digital threat neutralized, but the personal cost etched deep into his soul. In the cacophony of last night's violence, a quiet promise had been made—a promise that even in the darkest hours, hope could still flicker, however faintly.

Around him, the café hummed with life. Laughter and gentle chatter wove a tapestry of normalcy, starkly contrasting with the silence that now occupied the recesses of his thoughts. He watched as passersby, unaware of the night's terror, hurried along the cobblestone streets. For a brief moment, he allowed himself to feel the bittersweet irony of it all: the city was healing, yet he remained haunted by ghosts of the past.

*The Arrival of Julia*

Later that afternoon, as the sun began its slow descent behind the old Lyon skyline, the door of the café swung open. In walked Julia, dressed in a simple, yet elegant coat that hinted at both practicality and understated beauty. Her eyes, a mix of determination and resignation, scanned the room before settling on Mitrajjit. With measured steps, she approached the table where he sat, her presence commanding attention even in her quiet manner.

"Mitrajjit," she said softly, her voice carrying the weight of a thousand unspoken words. There was a gentleness in her tone that belied the hard edges of recent events—a vulnerability that spoke of the battles fought both externally and within her own heart. "I've been briefed. My current partner has been notified, and I must return to my duties soon. Our paths… they diverge now."

The words, delivered with a careful mix of regret and necessity, hung in the air between them. Mitrajjit rose slowly, each movement deliberate, as if to honor the gravity of the moment and the years that had led to this bittersweet farewell. His eyes, though steeled by countless missions and hardened by the passage of time, softened at her words, and memories of their past together flooded back in vivid detail.

"I understand," he replied quietly, his voice steady yet imbued with profound melancholy. "I will always cherish what we had, Julia. You saved my life tonight, in more ways than one." His admission was not just an acknowledgment of her actions on the battlefield—it was an homage to the love that had been their refuge amid chaos, the love that had lit even the darkest corridors of his existence.

For a long moment, they stood together in the fading light of day, the vibrant cityscape of Lyon stretching out behind them like a promise of new beginnings. The café, the river, the bustling streets—they all seemed to witness this poignant interlude, a delicate balance between duty and desire, between memory and the inexorable pull of the future.

### *An Intimate Farewell*

With a heavy heart, Julia reached out and gently touched Mitrajjit's arm. Her eyes, shimmering with unshed tears, held a depth of emotion that spoke of both love and loss. "I wish things were different," she whispered, her voice trembling as she confessed, "but my life has taken a different path. I'm carrying another man's child now. I have responsibilities, a future that I must honor." Her hand, resting tenderly over her slightly rounded belly, conveyed the quiet strength of a woman who had learned to balance love and sacrifice, hope and duty.

Mitrajit's gaze softened, and he stepped closer, his presence a silent assurance in the midst of his inner turmoil. "I never wanted to hold you back," he murmured, his words heavy with the sorrow of inevitable parting. "Our love, no matter how fiercely it burned, was always destined to be a beautiful, painful memory. But know this— nothing will ever erase what we shared. It will always be a part of me, a constant echo in every battle I fight."

They stood in the quiet of that intimate moment, surrounded by the gentle hum of the city beginning to settle into evening. The delicate interplay of light and shadow across their faces spoke volumes of the journey they had traversed together—a journey filled with passion, peril, and the kind of love that defies time and circumstance.

### *Promises in the Twilight*

As the conversation ebbed, the reality of their divergent paths pressed in on them once more. The duty to their respective causes was unyielding, a force that neither could escape. Julia's eyes, both hopeful and resigned, searched Mitrajjit's for one final assurance. "Promise me you'll come back to me," she pleaded softly, her voice imbued with a raw vulnerability that left him momentarily breathless. "Even if it means letting go of the past just enough to build a future—a future where we can at least remember the love we had."

Mitrajit's heart pounded with the enormity of the promise she sought—a promise that transcended the immediate demands of duty and ventured into the realm of hope. He took her hand in his, his grip firm and resolute. "I promise," he said, his voice steady despite the inner storm of conflicting emotions. "I will come back to you, Julia. When this mission is over and the city is safe, I'll find a way to return to the love that still burns within me."

Her eyes glistened with a mixture of gratitude and sorrow, and for a moment, the world around them receded until only the two of them remained—an island of fragile intimacy amid a sea of duty and sacrifice. They shared one final, lingering embrace, a touch that spoke of everything unspoken: the promise of a past that would forever haunt them, and the possibility of a future that, while uncertain, was worth every sacrifice.

*The Parting and the New Dawn*

As the final farewell drew near, Julia stepped back, her silhouette merging with the soft hues of the early evening crowd. She turned and began to walk away, her figure gradually blending into the throng of Lyon's bustling streets. The secret of her unborn child and the legacy of a love that could never be fully realized trailed behind her like an invisible cloak. Mitrajjit watched her disappear, a bittersweet smile tugging at his lips—a smile born of love, loss, and the unyielding hope that, in another life, they might find their way back to one another.

Standing alone in that quiet café, with the cool evening air wrapping around him, Mitrajjit felt a strange duality—a heaviness in his heart tempered by a growing sense of freedom. The final battle had been fought; the ghosts of the past had been exorcised through sacrifice and valor. Now, he would return to his duty, carrying with him the indelible mark of a love that had burned fiercely and left an everlasting imprint on his soul.

The café's ambient chatter resumed as twilight deepened, yet Mitrajjit remained ensconced in his private reverie. The city around him moved on—oblivious to the monumental battles fought in its shadow, unaware of the personal sacrifices that had paved the path to peace. He knew that the road ahead would be long and fraught with new challenges, but in the quiet spaces between heartbeats, he clung to the memory of Julia—a beacon of hope amid the darkness of duty.

As the last remnants of daylight faded and the city prepared for another night, Mitrajjit stood and slowly made his way out of the café. Every step was measured, every stride a silent vow that the love they had once shared would continue to guide him, even if it could never be reclaimed. With the ghost of Julia's touch still lingering on his skin and the promise of her return echoing in his heart, he stepped into the night—resolved to protect the city, to honor the past, and to build a future where even the deepest scars could one day give way to healing.

And so, with the memories of that final, bittersweet goodbye etched into his soul, Mitrajjit embraced the coming darkness—not as an end, but as the prelude to a new dawn, a new chapter where the legacy of love and sacrifice would forever be a part of who he was.

# Epilogue: A New Dawn

In the hushed, tentative hours before sunrise, Lyon stirred from a long night of turmoil. The city, still marked by the scars of violence and loss, now embraced a fragile peace that promised the slow return of hope. In a small, sparsely lit office overlooking the Rhône, Mitrajit sat at an old wooden desk, pen in hand, immersed in the final report of Operation Golden Crescent. Every carefully chosen word on the page bore the weight of valor and sorrow, a measured testament to a life spent protecting others while silently sacrificing personal happiness.

The report chronicled the night's fierce battles, the cold calculations of enemy strategies, and the heroic sacrifices that had saved countless lives. Yet, amid the precise language and detailed accounts of tactical maneuvers, there was an undercurrent of melancholy. Mitrajit's narrative was not merely a recitation of events; it was an elegy to the cost of duty—a record of what was lost in the relentless pursuit of peace. With each sentence, he revealed the endurance required to face both external enemies and the internal toll of a life lived in perpetual conflict.

As he scribbled the final lines, the quiet scratching of his pen on paper became a solitary rhythm, echoing the beat of his own heart. When at last he closed the file and submitted it to his superiors, a heavy stillness descended upon him—a moment of pause where duty and memory intertwined. Even as his report was filed away and the administrative hum of the organization resumed, his thoughts drifted unbidden to Julia.

Her image, soft yet indelible against the stark backdrop of danger and sacrifice, lingered in every fold of his mind. He recalled her luminous smile amid chaos, the steady glint in her eyes as she fought to save lives, and the tender moments they had shared in the midst of peril. Though fate had set them on diverging paths, her memory was a constant presence—an ember that refused to be extinguished by the bitter winds of duty.

Later that day, seeking solace from the relentless cadence of memories, Mitrajit wandered along the banks of the Rhône. The water, shimmering in the early light, mirrored the city's timeless beauty—a beauty forged by centuries of art, culture, and quiet sorrow. As he walked, the gentle murmur of the river mingled with the soft clatter of awakening footsteps, and the streets began to fill with the tentative stirrings of a new day.

Every step along the ancient promenade was a journey through time. He recalled the days when Lyon's narrow alleys had hidden clandestine meetings and secret promises. Now, as the first golden rays of the sun broke over the horizon, bathing the city in a warm, hopeful light, Mitrajit felt the stirring of something profound within him. In that radiant glow, he discovered a fragile promise: that even after the deepest darkness, new beginnings were possible.

Standing on a small stone bridge, he paused to take in the scene around him. The city was coming alive—shopkeepers opening their doors, locals greeting one another with soft smiles, and the gentle clink of coffee cups in bustling cafés. All these ordinary moments, seemingly trivial against the enormity of past events, now appeared as miracles of survival and resilience. Lyon, with all its timeless grace and hidden sorrows, had provided him with a bittersweet closure. The city's enduring spirit whispered that even the most broken hearts could mend, that hope could be reborn from the ruins of yesterday.

In a quiet, introspective moment, Mitrajit whispered to the awakening morning air, "Goodbye, Julia… and thank you." The words, simple yet laden with unspoken emotion, floated away on the breeze, carrying with them the echoes of a love that had transformed him. They were a farewell to what once was—a farewell to a love that had been both a sanctuary and a crucible. They were also a quiet promise to himself: that he would honor the memory of that love by moving forward, even if the scars remained.

As the day unfolded, Mitrajit's steps grew more resolute. He felt, deep within, that the final battle had been fought—not only against the tangible enemy but against the relentless ghosts of his own past. The sacrifices made on that dark night had exorcised some of the lingering demons that had haunted him for years. Yet, the price of victory was etched into every fiber of his being, a reminder that every act of courage came at a personal cost.

The memories of Julia, of her defiant spirit in the face of danger and her quiet grace under pressure, would forever be a part of him. They were no longer chains that bound him to a bygone era; instead, they were the embers of a fire that would continue to guide him forward. In the solitude of that new dawn, he resolved to let those memories serve as a beacon—a source of strength and inspiration, rather than a weight that held him back.

Returning from the riverbank, he made his way slowly through the awakening city. Each step was a measured blend of remembrance and determination. The lively chatter of passersby, the distant strains of street musicians, and the soft murmur of conversations filled the air, reminding him that life continued unabated even after unspeakable loss. Lyon was healing, and so, too, must he.

In the coming weeks, as the city rebuilt its shattered spirit, Mitrajit found solace in small, everyday acts. He reconnected with old friends, resumed quiet walks through familiar neighborhoods, and even allowed himself the rare luxury of laughter. Yet, in quiet moments of introspection—while watching a sunrise over the Rhône or while poring over the final details of another mission—his thoughts always returned to Julia. Her memory was a quiet refrain in the symphony of his life, a melody that, though tinged with sadness, also held the promise of redemption.

One crisp morning, as autumn leaves began to pepper the ancient streets of Lyon, Mitrajit visited the café where he had once sat alone by the river. Now, with time softening the edges of his grief, he sipped a warm cup of coffee and watched the world pass by with renewed clarity. The city had learned to live with its secrets, its scars, and its history, and he too had learned that even the most profound losses could pave the way for new beginnings.

In that gentle light, he penned a final, reflective note in his journal—a personal testament to the cost of duty and the price of love. He wrote of the battles fought, the sacrifices made, and the unyielding hope that even in the aftermath of darkness, the human spirit could rise again. His words were both a farewell to the pain of the past and a welcome to the promise of tomorrow—a declaration that, though he might forever carry the memory of lost love, it would no longer be a shackle to his heart.

With the city awakening around him and the promise of a bright new day on the horizon, Mitrajit closed his journal and stepped out into the soft, golden light of dawn. His heart, though scarred, beat with a renewed rhythm—a rhythm that acknowledged the past while boldly embracing the future. And as he walked along the banks of the Rhône one final time, his whisper carried on the breeze was not just a farewell, but also an expression of gratitude: "Goodbye, Julia... and thank you."

In that moment, as the day began anew, Mitrajit realized that every ending also held within it the seeds of a fresh start. The memories of lost love would forever guide him, not as chains that bound him to sorrow, but as cherished beacons lighting his way forward. With each step he took into the emerging day, he carried the legacy of that love—a legacy that would continue to shape him, inspire him, and, ultimately, free him from the darkness of yesterday.

Thus, beneath the radiant glow of a new dawn, Mitrajit embarked on the next chapter of his life—a chapter where duty and memory coexisted, where the lessons of the past nourished the promise of the future, and where every sunrise was a reminder that even the deepest scars could give way to healing and hope.

# About the Author

**Mitrajit Biswas**

Mitrajit Biswas is a versatile and emerging voice in contemporary literature, known for his ability to traverse diverse genres and themes, leaving a lasting impression on readers. His literary works span from graphic novels to historical fiction, and his storytelling is marked by a deep engagement with culture, change, and technology. Biswas is also an accomplished research scholar and academician. He holds Master's degrees in Commerce, specializing in Marketing, and in Philosophy. His academic pursuits are complemented by an active research profile, with interests in commerce, public relations, nation branding, global image management, and the socio-economic impacts of globalization. He has contributed to numerous scholarly publications, addressing topics such as sustainable development, the changing concept of statehood in Asia, the role of AI in organizational performance, and India's soft power on the global stage.

Mitrajit Biswas's writing is informed by his avid interest in history and foreign policy. He is passionate about exploring the intersections of historical events, geopolitics, and cultural narratives, both in his fiction and non-fiction work. His research papers and book chapters have been published in reputable journals and edited volumes, covering subjects like climate change policy, medical tourism, public diplomacy, and the geopolitical consequences of global conflicts. Biswas's literary style is characterized by a thoughtful blend of academic rigor and creative storytelling. He crafts narratives that are intellectually engaging while remaining accessible to a broad audience. His works often reflect a nuanced understanding of contemporary issues, drawing on his scholarly background to enrich his fiction with authenticity and depth. Beyond his writing and research, Mitrajit Biswas is an avid reader and a keen observer of historical trends and international affairs. His passion for history and geopolitics not only shapes his academic work but also inspires his creative endeavors, making him a distinctive figure in both literary and scholarly circles.

www.ingramcontent.com/pod-product-compliance
Lightning Source LLC
LaVergne TN
LVHW041556070526
838199LV00046B/1989